HELL HAS NO FURY

J.A. BEARS

INTRODUCTION

Betrayal is a wound that never heals. It festers and burns, demanding attention and seeking retribution. When trust shatters and loyalty morphs into lies, the world transforms into a battlefield where justice is no longer blind; it's merciless. In the shadows of broken promises, one soul rises, consumed by rage and haunted by secrets that claw at the edges of their sanity.

This is not a tale of heroes, but a harrowing descent into obsession, where vengeance becomes an all-consuming creed, and redemption drifts further out of reach. As darkness spreads, unraveling every truth and exposing the fragile nature of human relationships, one question looms: how far will you go when hell isn't a place, but a promise?

From the mind of J.A. Bears comes a gripping thriller that confronts the depths of despair and the quest for justice. As one person's journey unfolds amidst the ruins of trust, the lines between right and wrong blur, revealing how the pursuit of vengeance can transform the heart into a weapon.

HELL HAS NO FURY

It all started with a simple "hi" in a chatroom.

James was divorced, living alone, and just looking for someone to talk to. When Sierra replied, he was happy.

James sat in bed scrolling through his phone, hoping to find a woman to chat with. He had been divorced for a few years. The last woman he was with hadn't been marriage material, and after they broke up, he found out she'd been cheating on him with several other men. That discovery left James angry and distraught.

Trying to move on, he was surprised when a message popped up.

"Hi. 39 F here," Sierra wrote.

James smiled as they began to chat. They shared few details about each other. A former college football player, James had fallen out of shape over the years. Work and family life had taken their toll.

Their first chat lasted over an hour as they swapped stories and asked questions. When the topic of children came up, they both shared about their kids. But in the back of James's mind, he thought of the one he hadn't mentioned, the third child.

Before his divorce, James had an affair that resulted in another baby. He didn't spend much time with that child, though he did send the mother money every month.

Still, he enjoyed the conversation with Sierra. As their chat came to an end, Sierra typed, "Can we do this again tomorrow?"

"Sure," James replied. "What time are you available?"

"Around lunchtime," she answered. "Just make sure you use the same username and I will too."

James, not very good with technology, quickly grabbed a pen and paper to jot down her screen name.

"I got it," he typed. "I look forward to talking to you tomorrow."

"Me too," Sierra replied.

That night, James thought about their conversation. He wasn't proud of hiding the truth about his other child, but he told himself it probably didn't matter. After all, it was just a chatroom. Sure, it was where he'd met his last girlfriend, but what were the odds of that happening again?

The next day, James watched the clock closely as lunchtime approached. The moment it hit noon, he rushed to his car, logged in, and looked for Sierra.

She was already there. No sooner had he sent a message than she replied.

"I was looking for you," she wrote. "I'm happy you're here."

"So am I," James answered. "It's good to see you."

They spent the next two hours chatting. It became a daily routine, spilling over into weekends whenever she had time. Over the next few weeks, their bond grew stronger. Eventually, Sierra said it was time they started talking on the phone.

Just as she was about to send her number, she suddenly logged off.

James panicked. He didn't know where she'd gone or if she'd come back. He really liked her and had been looking forward to hearing her voice.

She had told him where she worked, so James searched online until he found the company number. He called and asked for her direct line, and, against the rules, they gave it to him.

He dialed. She answered.

"How did you get this number?" she asked, startled. "No one's supposed to have it."

"I know," James said. "You went offline, and I didn't see you come back. I did a little research and found it."

"You're crazy," Sierra said. "I was going to come back online."

"I didn't know when," James replied. "My lunch break was almost over. I didn't want to risk not talking to you again."

Sierra shook her head as he spoke.

"This is my number and now I have yours," she said. "I have to get back to work. You can text me later, and if I'm available, we can talk."

James's heart was racing. It had been a long time since he'd felt this excited about someone.

After the last one, he was pretty sure he wasn't going to be able to find another. After all, he was close to 50, with baggage. He had a decent job, but he wasn't wealthy by any means, as the divorce and the money he was giving for his other child kept things tight.

James went to the gym, came home, showered, and ate some dinner. He was nervous and excited, not knowing what was going to happen next.

About 9 p.m., James got up the nerve to send Sierra a text. "Hi, it's James. May I call?"

"No," Sierra responded. "I am busy with my youngest daughter." James's heart sank as he read it. He thought there was a real connection between the two of them.

"Can I call you back in about an hour?" Sierra typed out.

"Sure," James responded. "It will be great to hear your voice."

James sat up in bed, stunned, while his heart was pounding like a teenager. The way Sierra described herself, she sounded very pretty. She was 5 feet tall, with long black hair. She was a Caribbean woman and, from the sounds of it, had a very sexy body.

An hour later, James had a mile-wide smile as he saw a phone number from an area code he didn't know. But he knew it was Sierra.

"Hello," Sierra said.

"Hello," James replied. "It's good to hear your voice." Sierra had a bit of an accent, which James found very attractive.

"You too," Sierra replied.

For the next hour, the two of them talked. Their conversation covered a variety of subjects, from work to what they did in their free time. They laughed, but all the while, James couldn't believe he was talking to her.

He told Sierra about the two jobs he worked and that he was usually pretty busy, but it just happened to be a night when he was off.

As they wrapped up their conversation, Sierra told James, "You can text me in the morning. I am usually up pretty early because the girls have school."

"I will be more than happy to do so," James replied, not believing his luck in finding a woman like Sierra. "I look forward to hearing your voice, too."

"Me too," Sierra replied. "Good night."

"Good night," James said.

As James lay his head on his pillow, he imagined what she looked like. He loved the sound of her voice. As Sierra drifted off to sleep, she thought about how James sounded so nice. He may be a bit crazy because he did track her down, but she found it kind of romantic that he went through all that trouble just to get her number.

Over the next couple of weeks, the conversations became longer, and Sierra was becoming more comfortable with him. She asked him about the gym he worked out at, while she told him about her own gym. She asked if she could get a picture of him, and she would do the same.

The next morning, James went to the gym, having a bad hair day and a body beat up from college football. James still took the picture and sent it to her.

"Nice," Sierra responded. "Here's mine."

"Oh wow," James replied. "You look incredible."

"Thank you," Sierra responded.

"You are even more beautiful than I imagined," James said. "It matches your voice perfectly."

Sierra smiled at the compliments James showered on her. A very attractive woman, Sierra was picky when it came to men. After having a couple of relationships fail, Sierra decided that she was only going to date white men. They were far less likely to be a pain in the ass. She found them more attractive and less likely to be assholes.

After a few months of talking more, James's birthday came up.

Sierra texted him, telling him to have a happy birthday and that she was so happy he went looking for her that fateful day to get her number. She told him that she was running errands for the day but was going to talk to him later that night.

That night, as the two of them talked, James brought up the idea of the two of them meeting.

Sierra said that with the girls in school, she wasn't sure how it could happen, as she didn't have a lot of free time.

James mused and said, "OK, we will figure it out one day."

"I hope you had a great birthday," Sierra said.

"Talking to you made it one," James replied.

The two exchanged good nights, and as James turned onto his side to sleep, he thought about what he could do to see her. She was a far drive from where he lived, but he thought maybe something would come through as he fell asleep.

A few days later, James got some unexpected news from his company: there was a training session they wanted him to attend. Even better, it wasn't too far from where Sierra lived.

James could hardly wait to tell Sierra the good news at lunchtime. They talked every day at lunch for at least 20 minutes.

When James texted Sierra to ask if he could call, she said yes.

When she picked up, she could hear the excitement in his voice. "You aren't going to believe this," he said. "I'm going to be near you in a few weeks."

"What?!" Sierra exclaimed.

James explained that his company was sending him for training for a couple of days, and he wouldn't be too far from her. "Do you think you'll be able to meet me?" James asked.

"I think I can. What time will you be able to see me, and where will you be?" Sierra asked.

James told her that he had to attend dinner, but should be free around 8 p.m. "OK," Sierra said. "I will be there."

When the two of them hung up, they were both in disbelief that this was going to happen.

James could barely get through work the next couple of days as the two of them continued to talk. The anticipation of the meeting grew with each conversation. The sexual references they made to each other only heightened things even more. It had been a while for both of them.

Their first meeting went so beautifully, so naturally, that

within weeks James found himself packing up his life and moving to be closer to Sierra.

Sierra and her girls decorated and furnished the apartment. Their first Christmas together was magical as James adjusted to his new life.

The couple did things together; she introduced him to her family, and they all liked him.

Still, Sierra felt something was off with James, but couldn't put her finger on it. He was a little jumpy and didn't ask her to come inside with him when he went into his parents' house. She brushed it off as they made the long drive back home. After all, it was late when they showed up. Still, it bothered her.

Over the next few months, things seemed to be going well. James treated her with respect, spent time with her, and the sex was incredible. Whenever Sierra brought up James's oldest child and why they didn't speak, his response was always the same: "It was a messy divorce. Nothing more. Nothing less."

Sierra also noticed how guarded he was with his phone. Sometimes, she thought, a little too guarded. They continued their relationship, but as time went on, Sierra felt increasingly uneasy. Something was not right.

She had to find out what was going on with James. She did have him wrapped around her finger, as he was engrossed with her. They went out, and she spent the night with James a few times a month. James was consumed with work and trying to make her happy. But she still had an unsettling feeling.

She planned to try his phone, asking if he wanted to get a new one. The current phone he had was older; it wasn't as big, but she thought that if she could get it, it would tell all.

Sierra came up with the idea of using one of her girls' old phones, which was no longer in use. James took it to the company, but had trouble getting the information to transfer over. Sierra told him to give it to her, and she would handle it.

Later that day, Sierra called and asked for his passcode. James gave it to her and asked why she needed it. The sales guy had said it was to make sure all the information transferred over. When the first code didn't work, James thought for a moment and then gave her the correct passcode.

It worked, and a few minutes later, Sierra called and said, "I didn't look at anything. What is your life is your life."

It couldn't have been further from the truth, but James didn't catch it. He thought she was just being helpful.

"That motherfucker," Sierra said. "I knew he was lying to me."

Sierra was heartbroken and furious at the same time as she saw the pictures of James's other child, the one he had because of an affair. She saw the texts he sent, along with the money he was sending out.

That was the reason why his oldest didn't speak to him and why she had changed her last name. Sierra looked through all the texts he sent to the mother of his kids. The more she looked, the angrier she became.

This was a man she had given herself to, and he broke her trust.

Once she had her information, it was time to give him the punishment he deserved. She was livid. She found all this out just before her daughter's prom, but she would make it work. She started to plan what she needed to do to ruin and break him.

After all, she had warned him before that if he was misspeaking, she would ruin him, and none of it would come back to her.

While he was working out of town, Sierra called him and told him that she was trying to rent an expensive sports car for her daughter's prom. She said she needed $1,500 to clear her card so she could make the deposit. She knew James was going to do anything she wanted to keep her happy. She also knew that he didn't have that kind of money to give up right away, but he'd find a way.

James did find a way. The loan on his car was close to being paid off, but he refinanced it to get Sierra the money. It took a day or two, but he managed it. He gave her his card, and she paid it off. He didn't know that she already had the money, and he barely managed to put on a happy face as they took pictures the night of the prom.

Being completely clueless, James thought everything was going fine. Sierra was still calling him pet names, spending time with him, and giving updates on herself and the girls as time went on.

Gradually, Sierra started spending less time with him. He still had a car, but she knew his finances were beginning to stretch thin, thanks to the refinanced loan. In her mind, she needed to keep him in one place while draining his money.

She called a friend at a body shop and asked what she could do to take the car off the road and keep it in the garage for a while. She got the answer she wanted, and soon James found out.

On a Friday night, while Sierra was busy with herself and her girls, James was sleeping on the couch when he heard an alarm go off. It quickly subsided, but he got up, looked out the window, and didn't see anything.

He hadn't parked in his usual spot in front of the apartment, since another car was there. Instead, his car was around the corner, away from streetlights, and none of the nearby houses had cameras. Little did he know, Sierra had told the landlady of her plan and arranged for someone to park there. She contacted her brother-in-law, who was good with cars, and had him use a Sawzall to cut out the converter.

The next morning, when James came out to start his car

for work, he immediately heard a noise he knew wasn't right. He couldn't look underneath, but he recognized the sound from before. On his way to work, he called Sierra and told her his converter had been stolen. It was a common crime during the pandemic.

She took James to the collision shop, where they were very helpful. They told him they would do everything possible to get it fixed quickly. They also mentioned that they had known Sierra for a long time and would do anything to help her.

Since James was with her, he assumed it would be the same for him. Sierra simply told him it was bad luck as she drove him back to his apartment. She promised she would help take him to work and pick him up when she could.

At first, it went just as Sierra promised. She picked James up while taking the girls to the bus station and to school. Sometimes, they stopped for bagels. James went along for the ride, completely clueless about what was really happening. Sierra still kissed him, held his hand, and gave off the vibe that they were still a couple.

Sierra only told the people she needed to. She wasn't about to let anything slip, but she wasn't worried. James's head wasn't in the right frame of mind. His mother was battling health issues, and he was very worried about her. On top of that, not having a car and knowing his finances were getting tight weighed heavily on him.

As time went on, Sierra always had reasons why she

couldn't pick James up. Unable to rely on her, James started taking Ubers. At first, it wasn't bad, as he thought it would only be a few weeks until he got a new converter.

Sierra continued to watch and listen to his frustration as he waited for his car. All the while, she was enjoying it. She was careful with what she said, but the stress James carried was taking a toll. Plus, they were spending less time together, which made James even more distressed.

This gave Sierra more free time to start setting up connections, while still calling James just enough to make him think she was involved with him. She needed more time, and especially more money, since her Car lease was coming up.

She came over just enough and spent just enough time with James to keep him from suspecting anything. When he wanted sex, she gave in, but less frequently now, as she knew what he had done. She started pulling away gradually so he wouldn't notice. In her mind, she was already done with him.

James's birthday came and went. Sierra went out with him and back to his place for the night. When he asked her to stay the next morning, she made the excuse that she had to take her daughter to work. The truth was, she just wanted to be away from him.

While his car was still in the shop, Sierra made the pick-ups and drop-offs less frequent. Meanwhile, his account was being drained, and his credit cards were maxed out. To make things even more unbearable, he was stuck in his apartment, especially on weekends. He couldn't go to the gym, get groceries, or even go to work.

As time moved forward, Sierra watched James slowly start to crumble. He was still happy to be with her, but he told her how stuck he felt and how much he missed her. Even when he started his new position, it wasn't long before Sierra made her next move.

Months earlier, she had told him her pay was going to be cut because of the market, and she might need help when getting a new Car. Sierra even picked him up one Saturday to go shopping. She pretended to be annoyed that the salesman spent more time trying to woo James into buying it, and she complained about it on the way home.

When James asked if she was going to come back afterward, she responded with a short, "No, I'm not feeling well. My stomach is bothering me."

She went home, relaxed, and smiled to herself, knowing what her next step would be.

James's paycheck from his new position was quite a bit larger than before. Sierra congratulated him, but it only solidified her plan.

When she called James from the dealership on a Tuesday night, he was surprised, since she had told him she was going to take him. She said, "Darling, you know, since they cut my pay, can you help me make the down payment on the Car? I promise I'll pay it back."

James replied, "I think I can. How much do you need?"

"A thousand dollars," Sierra answered. "All I need is a picture of your card. Can you text it to me?"

"Will they take that?" James asked.

James could hear the salesman in the background, telling Sierra they would take it. Although money was tight for James, and Sierra had promised to repay him, he texted a picture of his card to her. Sierra smiled and said thank you to James, while she showed the picture to the salesman to charge the card for the deposit.

Of course, the card went through, and James asked Sierra to send him the receipt. She never did; she didn't want any proof he could use later in case he figured anything out.

The stress of the new job, his mother's health issues, and not having a car left James slowly starting to crack. Not seeing Sierra made things even worse for him, as he was lonely and trying to figure things out.

Sierra had James over for Thanksgiving dinner, but she didn't sit near him. She really didn't want any part of him, but she had to make it look like everything was normal. James said grace at the table, and the evening went along just fine.

For Sierra, it was another evening she had to endure with

him. At least she had the excuse of working, and James also had to work, which made things easier for her since he didn't have a car.

By the time Christmas came, James finally got his car back. Sierra had him come over later in the day. The less time she had to spend with him, the better. Without telling her family, they all exchanged gifts. Sierra went over the next night to stay with James as they exchanged gifts under the tree they had put up earlier in the month.

Even though Sierra told James she was going to help him take it down, she never came over. The New Year rang in with only a quick call at midnight to tell James she loved him. The calls were becoming less frequent.

She figured she would give him one more chance. She told him, "Let's make a trip. You can see your parents, and I can see my uncle." They made the long trip, and when James asked if she wanted to come up, she said no, she wasn't feeling well.

It struck James oddly as he made his way to his parents' house, but he didn't think much of it. He knew she was under a lot of stress. Her youngest was graduating in a few months, while her middle daughter was now a freshman in college. She always told him that she didn't like change.

On the way back home, Sierra told James that she was never going back to see her uncle. She said the trip was too much for her to take. James thought it was odd and asked if she was sure.

"Yes, I am," she replied sternly.

After they got back, the phone calls Sierra made to James became fewer and farther apart. When he asked if she was going to come over and help take down the Christmas tree, she replied angrily, "Take it down yourself."

James was confused and finally did it in the middle of April. He was missing her. He thought something was wrong, but he couldn't put his finger on it. When he tried to bring it up, he was met with sighs or groans.

When she finally gave in to come over, Sierra had already decided it was going to be the last time they were in bed together. James told her that he missed her company and that it wasn't always about sex, contrary to what Sierra had told him.

In June, Sierra's youngest daughter graduated. Her family was unaware of what she was doing. When they told James to get into the picture, Sierra's smile was firm. She knew this was going to be the final time he would appear in any pictures with her and her girls.

The next six months were torture for James. Barely talking to Sierra, he missed her deeply. He couldn't figure out what was going on. The new position was a lot more stressful than he had anticipated.

For his birthday, Sierra took him out for breakfast, and that was it for the rest of the day, as she had other plans. When he went back to see his parents and returned with a job offer, she acted shocked, so he decided to stay. Little did James know that she had hooked up with another man while he was gone.

Thanksgiving was just a morning trip for him, and that was it. There were times Sierra called James in the early evening to say that she and the girls were going out. He didn't hear from her for the rest of the night. He kept texting her good morning and good night, but she never responded. She only called at odd times, sometimes leaving him without contact for almost 18 hours.

What she was really doing was going out to see another man. She was done with James. On Christmas, it was over in an hour, and that was it. For New Year's, she went out and slept with a man she had met in the same chatroom where she had met James, while telling him she was going to her daughter's workplace.

With the new year barely underway, Sierra finally decided to break it off with him. She told him she was dealing with depression. When he asked if they were still going to be partners, she replied, "I don't think so."

It was the final straw, and James snapped. He started crying, asking why, and begging. The depression and loneliness he felt, along with the years of playing football, left him mentally and emotionally done.

He didn't think it was fair, but he couldn't think straight, and he knew he should have seen the signs. Sierra had told him that she had depression. That wasn't the case. Once her last child graduated from high school, in her mind, their relationship was over. She stopped saying "I love you" and told him that she was going through things.

But she was starting her new life, one in which she would never let a man control her. Not that James did, but she had given him her love and her family, and he had lied to her about his. She didn't doubt that he loved her, but he broke the one rule she had given him.

The weight she had put on, she started losing. She began meeting other men and was in control of who she was with. She did things with them that she never did with James. She even told a couple of them that she had a boyfriend, but in her mind, she wasn't cheating. When James confronted her shortly after the breakup, he told her that he had been recommended to get a test.

She played it off, crying, saying she would get her doctor to send her blood work. James didn't catch that it meant she was sleeping with other people, because it had been over six months since they were last together.

James was an emotional wreck. He was offered a job closer to home and knew he needed to take it. The thought of being around her was too much, but with his credit cards maxed out and little cash flow, he was fucked.

He was enraged and even packed the things he knew he

couldn't take back and brought them over to her. He placed them in front of the driveway so he couldn't be accused of trespassing.

He hoped it would get her attention, to show her how much he cared about her. It was the furthest thing from the truth for her.

He couldn't function at work, while Sierra just went along with her new lease on life. She met different men, gave them what they wanted, and got what she wanted. She slept with a vice president of a loan company, and he gladly put her on the payroll with a firm start date.

She even had a fake work profile to throw James off because she knew he was going to be looking for something. She didn't have to go to work and basically got paid vacation.

Every once in a while, James would show up in the chat room when she was in there, but she never answered him when he sent a message. She didn't want to give anything away. She knew James was going by the house and sometimes took her sister's car, leaving the Car at home.

One time, James drove by and texted her early Sunday morning. She told him the car was in the shop. But she was in bed with another man after making another conquest. There was nothing he could do to prove it.

Nothing could be attached to her. When James sent messages, she said "please stop" and that she was going through a lot. But he was looking for answers, and she didn't give him any. She just used the same response repeatedly.

One night, before James was going to move back home, he called the mother of his first two. He told her that he was going to die. He had taken a fair number of pills along with a couple of bottles of vodka.

He didn't want to die, but he couldn't think of a way out. He apologized to her for his affair and for not telling her the truth about it. He told her he was sorry for everything he had done. She accepted it, and it was enough to stop him from slicing his wrists. Instead, he took the end of the blade and drew blood from his forehead as the mother of his first two told him to just come back home. After passing out, fate intervened that morning when his new boss texted him to confirm his start date.

In his final week, James drove 4,000 miles to move everything he could. All the while, his landlady said it was in God's plan. On the final day, she told him that Sierra and her family were moving. But they weren't. It was just another way to get back at James.

Even when her husband asked if he had talked to Sierra, James gasped and replied that she hadn't talked to him in two weeks.

James sobbed as he left the area one last time, completely unaware of what was going on. He was destroyed, just what Sierra wanted. James barely got back to set up a new life, one without Sierra and in a place where he really didn't want to be.

He spent the first month wondering why she didn't block him if she hated him that much. He wondered why she didn't call to see if he made it back. Nothing made sense to him. After all, they had spent almost seven years together, the last six making sure they spoke to each other in the morning and at night. Once James started saying he loved her, almost every conversation ended that way, except for the last six months.

He went to therapy and was told to use adult coloring books to keep his mind busy. Instead, it gnawed at him. He wanted to get the closure he never got when he was put into an orphanage as a baby.

That scar he had carried throughout his life was ripped open when Sierra left him.

He couldn't understand what happened. After all, the first time James told her that he loved her, she replied that she already knew by the way he held her.

While he was struggling, Sierra told her family everything that happened and what was going on. The family was mad and upset, but they understood she was going to get hers.

When a friend of James's passed away unexpectedly a month later, James went on a four-day binge of drugs and alcohol. It got to the point where James called Sierra. Not knowing what he was saying or doing, he let loose a series of nasty words, which she remembered. It was something she would call upon in later texts.

Even when he confronted her about the no-show job, she said it was because she had a lot of friends. It was friends she slept with to get her power. She collected them like some people collect stamps. All of them were in her corner.

When he asked if she was seeing anyone, she replied, "Not that it's any of your business, but no."

It was true. She wasn't seeing just one person. She was seeing many different men. She wasn't lying.

She never intended to pay the money back, as it was the least he could give her after she had given herself and her family to him. She felt more than betrayed. She was disgusted and mad at herself for not trusting her first instincts. Furthering her anger was that her family liked him, even to the point that her aunt and uncle, whom they visited, told her to marry him.

It was the ultimate betrayal in her mind. He needed to pay, and pay in the worst way.

After months of James trying to figure out what happened, he had a dream, and it soon became a nightmarish reality.

He had given Sierra his phone, and not too long after that, everything started making sense. She wasn't suffering from depression; she was getting even. The phone, his car, the less time she was spending with him, she was playing the victim, but she was really the predator. It was all a front as she destroyed his life. She sent him back home broken and shattered. His family turned their back on him. His kids didn't want to talk to him.

Even after James had sent her messages showing that she had been with other men, she sent someone to text his phone and tell him that things were going to get messy if he didn't stop.

James finally realized why Sierra didn't block him after she ended things. She was going to use it as evidence and collateral if James got out of hand. She could play Miss Innocent, and with the connections she made, she was impenetrable.

"I told you several times why we are no longer together," she said. "Please stop texting me."

She knew that was only to cause him to react even more, but she was long over him.

Even when he had a car place look at his converter, he was told the wires were crossed. The mechanic said, "It's almost like someone did it on purpose." James didn't catch it at the time.

It finally all came together for James. He had fucked up and had no way out. There was only one thing left to do… make one final trip.

James prepared for his last ride. It was a drive he had made many times, either going to see Sierra or heading home. He made his final phone calls to the mothers of his children. He told them not to worry and that he loved his kids.

During the long drive through the night, James replayed everything in his head—from their first conversations to the first time seeing each other, to the bitter end he was facing.

Arriving early in the morning, he pulled up in front of her driveway, gun in hand, and waited. When he blocked her Car from getting out, she came out yelling at him. She told him it was all in his head and that it was over. No one was going to believe him anyway, because there was no proof. There wasn't anything he could do. She had his family's information, and with her connections, she could use her influence to have someone make a call to threaten or harm one of his children.

James raised the gun and pointed it at Sierra. Police sirens blared as they rushed to Sierra's house. James glared at her, the woman he truly loved but who had deceived him, standing in his sight. As police cars pulled up and got into position, James looked at her.

"You didn't have to do all of that to me, but I understand why you did," he said. "I truly did love you, but I was afraid to tell you the truth because you wouldn't see me anymore. I'm sorry."

With that, James turned to face the police, gun still in hand, and moments later, shots rang out. James's body took the bullets, and he crumpled to the street. As he took the first bullet, a sense of relief came over him. No longer was he running from anything anymore. The lies he told throughout the years were exposed, and he could finally rest. As he hit the street, he muttered how much he loved his kids, but he couldn't go on anymore because of Sierra.

As James's bullet-ridden body bloodied the street and commotion surrounded the neighborhood, Sierra stood over him, looking at him with disdain.

"I told you to never lie to me," she said.

ABOUT THE AUTHOR

Mr. Bears always had a way of telling stories to family and friends. Now he is putting them into words.

www.ingramcontent.com/pod-product-compliance
Lightning Source LLC
Chambersburg PA
CBHW060956120626
46557CB00003B/1195